D0490109

First published in Great Britain in 1999 by Andersen Press Ltd.,
20 Vauxhall Bridge Road, London SW1V 2SA. Published in Australia by
Random House Australia Pty., 20 Alfred Street, Milsons Point, Sydney, NSW 2061.
All rights reserved. Colour separated in Switzerland by Photolitho AG, Zürich.
Printed and bound in Italy by Grafiche AZ, Verona.

10   9   8   7   6   5   4   3   2   1

British Library Cataloguing in Publication Data available.
ISBN 0 86264 870 X

This book has been printed on acid-free paper

THE LITTLE
RED HEN

retold and illustrated by

MICHAEL FOREMAN

Ⓐ

Andersen Press
London

Down the road and over the hills
lived a little red hen. She lived in
a farmyard with the farm dog,
the farm cat and a big, fat pig.
"Oink! Oink!"

One day, when the little red hen was out walking, she found some grains of wheat. She gathered them up and carried them back to the farmyard.

"Who will help me plant this wheat?"
she asked.

"Not I," said the dog.
"Not I," said the cat.
"Not I," said the big fat pig.
"Oink Oink!"

"Then I shall do it myself,"
clucked the little red hen.

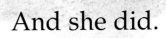

And she did.

The little red hen cared for the wheat
until it grew tall and golden.
"Who will help me cut the wheat?"
she asked.

"Not I," said the dog.
"Not I," said the cat.
"Not I," said the big fat pig.
"Oink, oink!"

"Then I shall do it myself,"
clucked the little red hen.
And she did.

"Now who will help me carry this wheat to the mill, to be ground into flour?" asked the little red hen.

"Not I," said the dog.
"Not I," said the cat.
"Not I," said the big fat pig.
"Oink, oink!"

"Then I shall do it myself,"
said the little red hen.
And she did.

The miller ground the wheat into flour
and put it in a sack, and the little red hen
dragged the sack back to the farmyard.

"Who will help me carry this flour
to the baker, to be baked into bread?"
asked the little red hen.

"Not I," said the dog.
"Not I," said the cat.
"You carried it here all right, so you can
carry it to the baker," said the big fat pig.
"*Oink, oink!*"

"And so I shall,"
clucked the little red hen.
And she did.

The baker made the flour into
a wonderful big loaf that smelled of
sunshine and poppies and the little red hen
carried it back to the farmyard.
"Who will help me eat this bread ?"
she asked.

"I will!" said the dog.
"I will!" said the cat.
"I will!" said the big fat pig.
"Oink, oink!"

"Oh no, you will not!" clucked the little red hen.
"I have some *new* friends coming for tea!"

And she did!

Oink, oink!